Warpath 4
Depth-charge Danger

'Range?' asked the commander.

'Three and a half miles and closing,' said the sonar operator. 'Three and a quarter. Three miles. Two and three-quarters –'

'Ready –' Perry ordered.

'Two and a half –'

'Fire!'

There was a hiss and our submarine recoiled in the water as a torpedo was discharged.

'Incoming enemy torpedo!' came a warning shout from the sonar operator.

Read and collect the other books in the
Warpath *series*

1: TANK ATTACK
2: DEADLY SKIES
3: BEHIND ENEMY LINES

WARPATH 4
Depth-charge Danger

J. ELDRIDGE

A fictional story
based on real-life events

PUFFIN BOOKS

With thanks to Wing Commander Ron Finch

PUFFIN BOOKS

Published by the Penguin Group
Penguin Books Ltd, 27 Wrights Lane, London W8 5TZ, England
Penguin Putnam Inc., 375 Hudson Street, New York, New York 10014, USA
Penguin Books Australia Ltd, Ringwood, Victoria, Australia
Penguin Books Canada Ltd, 10 Alcorn Avenue, Toronto, Ontario, Canada M4V 3B2
Penguin Books (NZ) Ltd, Private Bag 102902, NSMC, Auckland, New Zealand

On the World Wide Web at: www.penguin.com

Penguin Books Ltd, Registered Offices: Harmondsworth, Middlesex, England

First published 1999
3 5 7 9 10 8 6 4

Text copyright © J. Eldridge, 1999
Photographs © the Imperial War Museum
All rights reserved

Set in Bookman Old Style by Rowland Phototypesetting Ltd,
Bury St Edmunds, Suffolk

Made and printed in England by Clays Ltd, St Ives plc

British Library Cataloguing in Publication Data
A CIP catalogue record for this book is available from the British Library

ISBN 0-141-30240-2

Contents

The Battle in the North Atlantic   1
Route to Norway   4
Submariners' Menu   5

Chapter 1: Under Attack   7
Chapter 2: Damaged   11
Chapter 3: Old Friends   16
Chapter 4: Briefing   22
Chapter 5: The X-craft   31
Chapter 6: Setting Sail   37
Chapter 7: Sunk   45
Chapter 8: Norway   50

British and German Submarines
    of World War Two   56
The German Battleship *Tirpitz*   63

Chapter 9: Through the Minefield   64
Chapter 10: Tragedy   73
Chapter 11: Caught in the Nets   79
Chapter 12: Bombs Away   85
Chapter 13: Target!   90
Chapter 14: Short of Oxygen   95
Chapter 15: Going Down   101

Author's Note   108
What Happened Next?   110
X-craft Attack Route   112
Tirpitz in Norway   113
Inside the X-craft   114

The Battle in the North Atlantic

At the start of the Second World War Britain had a ten to one warship superiority over Germany. But this advantage was misleading: many of Britain's ships were old and coming to the end of their serviceable lives. However, most of Germany's vessels were of modern design and construction. The prize possessions of the German Navy were the *Bismarck* and the *Tirpitz*. These sister battleships, with their specially strengthened hull armour, were the mightiest warships afloat at the time. The British warships, with their thinner hulls, would have been at a disadvantage in any major sea battle with these two giants.

The *Bismarck* was sunk by the British

Navy in May 1941 after a long battle on the open seas against a superior number of British ships. The Germans learnt a valuable lesson from that defeat and, as a result, they moored the *Tirpitz* in the safety of the Norwegian fjords, ready to attack Allied convoys when needed.

The ever-constant threat posed by the presence of the *Tirpitz* and two other heavy battleships, *Scharnhorst* and *Lützow*, caused major problems for the British Navy. A huge part of the British fleet was put on stand-by in the North Atlantic, ready to take on the mighty enemy battleships. Also, no Allied convoy was safe while these battleships were seaworthy.

The RAF launched a number of air attacks at the *Tirpitz*, but she was protected by the high sides and narrow approaches to the fjords and by strong anti-aircraft defences. All these strikes failed.

Surface assaults from the sea were out of the question because of the superior power of the *Tirpitz*'s armaments and its natural protection from the fjords. An attack by conventional submarines was also impossible because the entrances to the fjords that housed the *Tirpitz* were protected by two layers of heavy metal netting suspended in the water – one anti-submarine, the other anti-torpedo.

In October 1942 the Royal Navy sent out a small fleet of 'Chariots' (unarmed torpedoes that could carry two divers). The plan was to attach limpet mines to the *Tirpitz*'s hull. This attack also failed.

The *Tirpitz* seemed to be invincible.

Meanwhile, the battle in the North Atlantic raged. Allied shipping losses mounted as a result of German U-boats hunting in 'wolf packs'. British submarines went to protect the convoys bringing vital supplies to the last free islands of Nazi-dominated Europe. The German Navy and Air Force – protected by the threat of the giant *Tirpitz* – in turn set out to hunt and destroy the British submarines.

By spring 1943 the Allies appeared to be losing the war of the North Atlantic; May of that year was to be the turning-point.

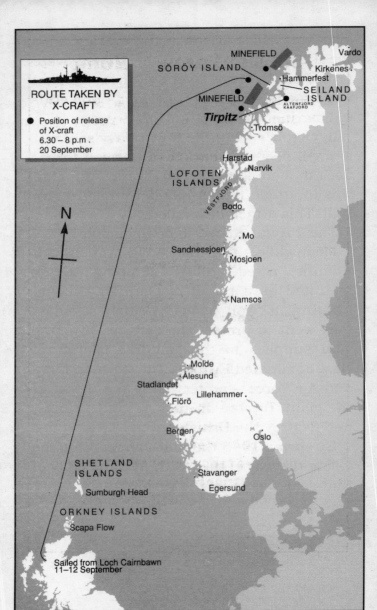

Submariners' Menu

A typical day's food on a British
World War Two submarine.

Breakfast
Grapefruit
Fried Fish

Lunch
Tinned Soup
Corned Beef
Pickles
Baked Beans
Cheese and biscuits

Tea
Marmite

Dinner
Pea Soup
Beef Steak Pudding
Boiled Potatoes
Tinned Carrots
Tinned fruit and custard

They said the *Tirpitz* was unsinkable. I was going to find out if they were right.

Lieutenant John Smith
Commanding Officer
X-craft 1943

Chapter 1

Under Attack

KERRBOOOOOOSHHHHH!
The force of the exploding depth-charge hurled our submarine violently sideways. I grabbed frantically on to the periscope housing to stop myself being thrown against the metal walls.

Commander Walters gestured for everyone to stay silent. We knew that the two German ships above would be listening out for us with their hydrophones. No one dared to move in case they made a noise.

Kerboooooooooshhhhhhhh!

Another explosion, but further away this time. The submarine rocked as the force of the blast pushed us backwards through the water.

Chief Stannard, our petty officer, winked at me confidently. I didn't feel so optimistic. Here I was, Lieutenant John Smith, twenty years old, on my third voyage in the submarine *Sandtail*, trapped between the Germans sixty feet above and the icy depths below. My first two voyages had been without major incident. We'd gone home empty-handed after the first, and had sunk two tankers on the second. This third trip we had ventured almost up to the Norwegian coast, where we'd had major successes, sinking four supply ships.

In retaliation the Germans had sent out spotter planes and anti-submarine craft to look for us. Two hours earlier a Dornier bomber had spotted us cruising just below the surface of the water and had dropped depth-charges. The charges had been set too deep. In one way this was fortunate because they exploded far beneath us. However, the explosions were strong enough to push the sub sharply to the surface. Our Number One, Derek Anderson, flooded all the tanks with ballast as fast as he could, to keep us beneath the surface of the water, but it was no good. We had

con...
finis...

We
and b...
avoid
periscop...
Walters
ships comi...

With no p...
bombardmen...
way of know...
couldn't hit t...   ...es.
Firing torpedoes   ...ny reveal
our position to th...   ...mander Walters
ordered the engine shut off and silence to
be maintained. In the three hours since
then no man had said a word.

We just sat deep beneath the waters of
the North Atlantic and waited while depth-
charges dropped. Some had been very
near, the later ones further away. We were
thinking the worst was over when . . .

KABOOOMMMMMMMMMMMMMM!

An immense explosion rocked the sub.
The air pressure began to soar as we sank
deeper. We were now well beyond the
water pressure this sub was designed to

dive soon

ry lighting failed
ged into complete

Chapter 2
Damaged

As I sat there in the pitch black I thought: *This is it. We're going to die.*

'Start engines!' ordered Commander Walters. 'Blow main ballast tanks!'

There was no other choice. Below us lay only death; above us, at least, there was a chance of survival.

In the darkness we worked by touch and memory. A torch came on as the coxswain, Ian Bailey, found his feet. The engineers cursed as they tried to fire up the diesel engines, but the high level of carbon dioxide in the submarine had slowed down the starting process.

Meanwhile we struggled to vent the main ballast tanks by hand. We knew it would send tell-tale bubbles to the surface, but we hoped they'd be lost among the turbulence thrown up by the depth-charges.

The hull of the submarine creaked and groaned under the pressure. At any second I expected the metal frame to give way and the sea to pour in.

Then the engines kicked into life.

'Take us up!' snapped Commander Walters.

The hull of the *Sandtail* groaned and screamed as we levelled out. The sound of air whistled through the sub as the ballast tanks emptied. Finally we were on an even keel again.

I checked the depth-gauge, but it was out of action. The pressure of the sudden dive had been too much for it.

'Set course six zero five!' ordered Walters.

'Course set six zero five,' repeated the helmsman.

All the time we waited for another explosion.

'I counted twenty-four,' commented Chief Petty Officer Stannard.

We all knew what he meant. The smaller

German ships usually carried ten depth-charges each. That meant a total of twenty depth-charges would have come down from them. The real question was, how many depth-charges had the Dornier carried? Were there more to come? We were obviously lucky. No more explosions followed. The sea fell silent. And so, leaking, battle-scarred and with no periscopes, we limped our way home.

For the last leg of the journey back to base at Montrose, on the east coast of Scotland, we sailed on the surface, with Commander Walters directing operations from the conning-tower. The attack had smashed the periscopes and destroyed our wireless aerials, so under the surface we would have been helpless. We were a sorry sight. With water leaking in from cracks in the hull, it was obvious that the *Sandtail* would need an extensive refit before she could return to active service.

On the first night back on land, I was sitting in the quarters I shared with my friend, Jimmy Ferguson, the *Sandtail*'s Third Officer, discussing what would happen to us now we were without a boat, when there was a knock at our door.

Jimmy opened it to reveal a motorbike messenger dressed in waterproofs and still wearing his goggles and leather helmet.

'Lieutenant Smith?' he asked.

'That's me,' I said.

'Orders for you, sir.'

I took the envelope from him and waited till he'd gone before opening it. It was an official-looking brown envelope with official-looking marks on it, but the message inside had been scribbled on a scrap of paper: Lieutenant John Smith to report to Invervegain Base, Loch Striven, 10th August.

Jimmy saw the puzzled frown on my face and grinned. 'Let me guess: the Admiralty have promoted you to captain?'

I handed him the scrap of paper. He read it and shrugged, obviously as puzzled as I was.

'Loch Striven,' he mused. 'Isn't that where those odd experiments are going on?'

'What odd experiments? Chemical weapons? I don't fancy being used as a guinea-pig in any kind of experiment.'

'No. Some peculiar sort of boat some-one's invented. It's supposed to be a secret.'

'If it's supposed to be a secret how do you know about it?' I asked.

'I've got an uncle who works on the River Clyde. He and his workmates saw some strange craft being put through its paces. Let's face it, a submarine – even a midget one – isn't something you can hide easily.'

I was intrigued. 'A midget submarine?'

'That's what Uncle Baxter thought it looked like. But then, Uncle Baxter also thinks he saw the monster in Loch Ness, so you have to take what he says with a pinch of salt.' Jimmy grinned again. 'Anyway, lucky you.'

'Why lucky?' I asked.

'Well, you'll actually get to find out what's going on there and see what this mystery is all about. Who knows, the top brass might be trying to trap Nessie herself to use against the Germans. You might be going up there to catch the Loch Ness Monster!'

Chapter 3
Old Friends

Two days later I arrived, as ordered, at Invervegain Base on Loch Striven on the Firth of Clyde. The first person I saw as I walked through the gates was an old friend from naval college, Peter Redford. Like me, he was a lieutenant who'd gone into submarines.

'John!' he greeted me cheerily. 'Don't tell me they've roped you in on this as well!'

'Roped me in on what?' I asked.

Peter winked at me mysteriously. 'Top secret,' he said. Then he laughed and added, 'Except about half the population of the Firth of Clyde knows about them because they look so peculiar, and no one thinks they will ever work properly.'

'What are you talking about?' I asked. I

hazarded a guess, remembering what Jimmy Ferguson had told me. 'Midget submarines?'

Peter laughed again. 'See, even you've heard about them! It shows just how secret they are! But don't worry, I'm sure the Germans won't be interested. Like I say, no one expects them to work. Not on long journeys anyway. Nothing further than Glasgow! Anyway, come and have a cup of tea and you can tell me what's been happening to you since I last saw you. Lost any good submarines lately?'

I was curious to see these midget submarines that everyone seemed to know about and was tempted to ask Peter if he'd show me them, but instead I decided to join him in his offer of a chat over a cup of tea. It had been at least a year since I'd last seen him and there's nothing that submariners like more than getting together and swapping stories about life beneath the waves.

I followed Peter along the quayside to a group of battered old buildings. From one of them wafted the smell of tea brewing.

'This is it,' said Peter. 'The worst sandwiches and the lousiest tea in Britain. But when you're hungry and thirsty, it seems like manna from heaven.'

We went in and found ourselves a table and Peter brought us over a mug of tea each. He'd been right: the tea was awful. It was thick, brown and sludge-like. I shrugged in cheerful resignation as I sipped at it.

'I expect it's not their fault,' I said. 'It's the shortages caused by the war. They've had to use the cheapest sort of tea leaves.'

'These aren't tea leaves – this is made from tea dust,' said Peter. 'This has nothing to do with the war. I bet you this place always made terrible sandwiches and awful tea. Well, how are you? I ran into Jerry Kent and he said you'd had a spot of bother. Lost your boat.'

'Jerry is exaggerating, as he always did. We ran into problems out near the Norwegian coast and as a result the *Sandtail*'s in for a refit. Nothing wrong with her that a bit of welding and a few coats of paint won't put right.'

'And a couple of new periscopes, from what Jerry says,' grinned Peter.

I shrugged. 'All right, there was some structural damage, but we got four German ships, so we didn't do too badly. How about you?'

Peter pushed back the lock of fair hair that fell across his eyes. It was a mannerism of his that I remembered from naval college. Even when he had his hair cut very short, he still put his hand up and pushed it back.

'Me? Well, after we did our training I got a commission on the *Swallow*. Trim little craft, one of the S-types, but old.'

'The *Swallow*?' I said. 'I heard you were on the *Swordfish*.'

Peter nodded. 'That was afterwards. After we were sunk in the *Swallow*.' He shook his head, and for once his usual cheerfulness vanished. 'A bad business. We hit the bottom, way down. Lost eight men.'

'What happened?' I asked.

'U-boat,' said Peter. 'Luckily for us it was on its own and not in a pack, or we'd all have bought it.' He shrugged airily, dismissing it. 'So, that was it. I was patched up back at base and then sent out on the

Swordfish, where I was very happy, until I got the call to come up here.'

'To the secret mission that's so top secret that half of Scotland knows about it,' I commented sarcastically.

'Oh, the mission's secret enough,' said Peter. 'And believe me, I've been trying hard to find out what it is, but no one is saying anything. All we can guess is that it's to do with looking for something in the Scottish lochs. After all, I've seen these midget subs and I can't believe they can get very far under their own power.'

I frowned. A thought had just come into my head.

'What's the matter?' asked Peter.

'I'm thinking about the Chariots. You know, the human torpedoes. A bit larger than a torpedo with a couple of divers riding on it. Maybe this is another version?'

Peter thought about it for a moment and then his face broke into a broad grin. 'Do you know, John, I think you may have hit it! It makes more sense than bringing experienced submarine officers all the way up here just to do some exploring locally.

And if you are right, it means that we could be sent anywhere in the world.'

I sipped the tea and thought about it seriously, and then suddenly the realization struck me. 'Not just anywhere, Peter, I think I know just where we're going.'

'Where?' he asked, intrigued.

'A place where not one of this country's armed forces – not the navy, not the air force, not the army, nor the Commandos – has been able to get to so far. I think we're being sent right into the lion's den.'

'Where?' asked Peter again, still puzzled.

'The fjords of Norway. I think they're sending us to sink the *Tirpitz*.'

Chapter 4
Briefing

We assembled in the briefing room just before 0800 hours the next day. There were twenty of us, sitting at individual desks as if we were back at school. Apart from Peter, I knew just two of the others: Daniel Cartwright and Edgar Wood. They'd also been at naval college with Peter and myself, but in the year ahead of us. The other sixteen men waiting quietly at their desks were a mixed bunch. A couple were in their early thirties, most in their early to mid-twenties. I guessed that Peter and I, at twenty, were about the youngest.

At 0800 on the dot, the door to the briefing room opened and the voice of the Number One snapped out, "Tenshun!"

We all sprang smartly to our feet as a

small bearded figure strode into the room and took his place in front of us. Rear-Admiral Pike.

'At ease,' he said. 'You may sit.' He surveyed us for a second before continuing. 'You are all here because you volunteered for special services. It is time for that volunteering to be turned to good use.'

The rear-admiral unrolled a picture and tacked it to the board. A buzz went round the room as we saw that it showed a very small submarine. What made it unusual was the lack of a conning-tower, instead it had a small hatch opening at the top.

'By now you will all have heard rumours about our new secret weapon, which means it is no longer a secret,' he said wryly. 'This, gentlemen, is the X-craft, a midget submarine that holds a crew of four: a commander, navigator, engineer and a diver. You are now X-craft crew members. Later your commanding officer will be allocating you to your crafts. My task is to inform you of your mission.'

Rear-Admiral Pike moved across to a map of Europe on the wall and tapped the coast of Norway.

'Hidden in a fjord here is the German battleship *Tirpitz*.'

At this Peter turned to me and winked. Pike saw this and snapped acidly, 'Is there something the matter with your eye, young man?'

'No, sir,' said Peter crisply.

'Then kindly pay attention.'

I resisted the strong temptation to smile at Peter's being told off.

Pike moved away from the map and began to pace around in front of us.

'There is no need for me to tell you about the havoc that the *Tirpitz* is causing to our ships in the Atlantic. The RAF have tried bombing her – with no success. Last year we tried using a team of Chariots to mine her. Some of you were involved in that mission and I know how bitterly you felt its failure. Well, this time there is going to be *no* failure. This time we are going to sink the *Tirpitz*, and you are the men who are going to do it!'

I shot a quick look at the faces of the men around me. So some of them had been out there before. I looked forward to talking to them afterwards and getting the inside story on those 'human torpe-does'.

Rear-Admiral Pike continued the brief-ing. 'We are sending out five X-crafts. Each one will be towed behind a regular S-class submarine. A caretaker skeleton crew of three will be in each X-craft on the outward journey to keep it operational. You gentlemen will have the luxury of being passengers on the S-subs on your way to Norway. Once the fleet is within range of the Norwegian coast, you will transfer to your X-crafts to carry out the mission.

'Because these craft are very small there has been no room for things like radios. Once you have set out in them you will not be able to communicate with each other, or with anyone else. You will be on your own.'

Pike tapped the picture of the tiny sub. 'You have one periscope. You also have three glass viewing ports above and at each side of the commander's position in the control room. The periscope and view-ing ports are your only contact with the outside world, other than your diver, whose job it will be to cut a way through the anti-submarine nets that bar the way to the fjord.

'Each X-craft is armed with two two-ton charges, each situated in a casing on either side of the sub. Your job is to place those charges beneath the *Tirpitz*. You will need to co-ordinate the timing so that you don't blow each other up.'

He looked at his watch, and then announced: 'The final details of your mission will be given to you on your way to Norway. In the meantime, I suggest you get acquainted with your new craft.' He looked at Number One, who was still standing stiffly to attention by the door. 'Number One, give them their crew allocations and take them out to see their new homes.'

Number One took over at the front of the room.

'The midget subs have been designated X5, X6, X7, X8 and X11,' he announced.

'I wonder what happened to X9 and X10,' I whispered to Peter as Number One turned to the blackboard and began writing our names on it in chalk.

'Sank due to mechanical problems, so I

hear,' Peter whispered back. 'Apparently they've had a lot of teething troubles with these things.'

We watched as our names went up. Peter had been put in charge of X5, and I was in charge of X11. Even though it was just a four-man boat, X11 was my very first command.

Number One got us five commanders to stand out front and then called out the rest of our crews to join us. My men were Eric Stevens (who was to be the navigator), James Munro (the engineer and helmsman) and Bill Watson (our diver). There was no time for proper introductions, merely a nod at each other as each man stepped out to join me.

'Right,' announced Number One. 'You've met each other, now come along and meet your craft.'

As I walked along the quayside with my crew I couldn't help feeling rather a fraud. Here I was, twenty years old and in command of men older than me and much wiser in the ways of the sea.

Eric Stevens – stocky, tough, blond-haired – was Australian, about nine years older than me. He'd once had a deep tan, but his time in submarines had led to it starting to fade. He was cheery soul and even as we walked I could hear him telling a joke to Bill Watson. Watson was from Toronto, Canada. We certainly were an international crew on X11: one Englishman, one Australian, one Canadian and a Scot.

'So the Germans caught these prisoners of war escaping from their camp,' said Stevens. 'The camp *Kommandant* lined them all up and told them, "Vot you haff done is a serious crime against the Reich and you all deserve to be shot! However, I am a kind and gentle man, so instead I shall be sending you to ozzer camps. Half of you will be going to Poland and ze ozzer half will be going to Germany." The *Kommandant* paused before adding, "The top half of you will be going to Poland, and the bottom half to Germany!"'

Watson joined in Stevens' laughter as they walked along side by side. I noticed that the fourth member of our crew, James Munro, didn't join in. He was a tall red-haired Scot. Too tall, one would have thought, to have fitted comfortably inside a submarine. I moved alongside and fell into step with him.

'Stevens is a bundle of laughs, isn't he?' I commented.

'Some things shouldn't be laughed at, sir, if you want my opinion,' replied Munro with a scowl. 'People being killed by the Germans is one of them.'

'I think Stevens is just trying to relieve the tension,' I said, hoping to pour oil on troubled waters. The last thing I wanted was my crew members at loggerheads with each other.

'Mebbe. Still, I don't think it's a thing to make jokes about. Some of us have lost friends and family in this war.'

'I'm sure Stevens means no harm,' I said. 'After all, think how far he's come to fight this war. Halfway across the world. If he'd wanted, I'm certain he could have stayed safely at home in Australia.'

This time I'd said the right thing. Munro looked at Stevens as he chatted to Watson and nodded. 'Aye, I never thought of it like that.'

'I was just thinking about something

that Rear-Admiral Pike said back at the briefing,' I said, trying to turn the conversation.

'Aye?' said Munro. 'Which bit would that be, sir?'

'About the Chariots expedition last year. It seems some of our team were on it. Do you know who?'

Munro nodded, and once more the expression on his face hardened. 'Aye, I went out with my brother Robert on that mission.' His face darkened with a mixture of sadness and anger as he added, 'I came back. He didn't.'

Chapter 5
The X-craft

I didn't ask Munro anything further about the failed Chariots mission; I was sure he would tell me all about it in his own good time.

By now we had reached the far end of the quay, and there in front of us were five of the smallest submarines I had ever seen. They looked almost like toys.

'There you are,' announced Number One. 'Climb aboard and take a look.'

As commanding officer I was first to climb down the hatchway into X11. To call it a midget submarine was no exaggeration. The whole thing was about fifty feet long on the outside. There was no room to stand up anywhere inside it, let alone to move from side to side easily. Inside, the pressure hull was about five and a half feet in diameter at its widest point, and from there it tapered to either end, fore and aft. The deck was also raised six inches from the bottom, cramping the space even further.

The four of us were soon pressed together inside the craft, shoulders slumped in a stoop.

'My first act as commanding officer of the X11,' I announced, 'is to order you all to sit down before we knock ourselves out trying to move around.'

We sat down at our stations in the tiny control room. My position was by the periscope, right in the centre. Stevens, acting as first lieutenant, was just behind me at the hydroplane, pump and motor controls. Munro was in front of me at the steering. Watson sat where he could find a space near to the watertight door to the Wet and Dry room, or W & D room for short. This was between the cramped control room and the forward compartment. When the W & D room was flooded, Watson would be able to open the hatch to get out of the sub once the time came for him to cut the anti-submarine nets.

The forward compartment was also a tiny space. It housed the fuel tanks and batteries. At the rear was the aft compartment where the engine and motor were housed.

Either side of the control room was a large lever. These levers opened the two outside bays, one each side of the hull, to drop the explosive charges underneath *Tirpitz*.

The four of us sat there, looking around the tiny sub. We had all been in cramped submarine quarters before, but this X-craft was a whole new experience: it was like being in a sardine tin. We could touch each other from our positions without stretching.

'Neat,' commented Stevens. 'Everything's here. And you don't have to walk around to get it. Very energy-saving.'

'If the Germans pick these things up on their sonar they'll just think we're a shoal of fish,' grinned Watson.

I tested the periscope.

'Well, skipper?' asked Stevens. 'What's the vision like?'

'After the periscopes I've been used to,

this is like looking through the bottom of a beer bottle,' I complained. 'Still, it'll have to do and at least we've got the viewing ports as well.'

'So long as we make it to Norway,' grunted Munro. 'We'll finish the job from there.'

For the next few days we tested the X-crafts, taking them up and down Loch Striven. They were slow, with maximum speed on the surface of 6 knots and about 5 knots submerged. Not that speed was that important on our mission. Operation *Tirpitz* was all about us being able to sneak our way past the German defences and up into the fjord where *Tirpitz* was berthed.

The night before we were due to set sail, I sat in the Officers' Mess with Peter and the other commanders: Daniel Cartwright, Edgar Wood and an Australian, Stephen Pitcher. All of us joked about the lack of space inside the tiny experimental subs and how there was no room inside them to stroke a cat, let alone to swing one.

'The chaps I feel sorry for are the care-taker crews,' commented Daniel, in between sipping his beer. 'After all, we only have to spend a couple of days in them once we get to the Norwegian coast. Those poor chaps will be in them for over a week. Can you imagine? A whole week cramped up in one of those things. Let's hope they all get on with each other.'

'Hmm,' murmured Stephen, 'there's one thing that no one's mentioned yet.'

'What's that?' asked Peter.

'Well, we've all agreed these things aren't made for speed. They're also not made for long-distance travel, which is why they're being towed all the way across the Atlantic.'

'Correct in every way,' nodded Edgar. 'Give that man a coconut.'

'So,' continued Stephen, his eyes twinkling mischievously, 'the question that comes to my mind is: does anyone know how we get back?'

We all sat silent for a moment, realizing that it was the one question none of us had thought about.

'They're sure to keep the S-subs waiting for us,' said Daniel confidently.

'Even if the Germans attack us once

they find out what's going on?' mused Stephen. 'Like after we've sunk the *Tirpitz*, for example?'

'They'll wait for us as long as they can,' put in Edgar. 'Of that I'm sure.'

'So am I,' said Peter confidently. With that he raised his glass in a toast: 'To the sinking of the *Tirpitz*!'

Chapter 6
Setting Sail

At 0600 the next morning we left port. Ahead of us was a journey of 1,500 miles across rough and icy seas full of potential dangers – floating mines, packs of German U-boats, anti-submarine patrol boats, enemy destroyers and aircraft laden with depth-charges ready to bomb us as soon as they saw our shapes beneath the waves.

We travelled in a convoy of five submarines. Myself and the crew of X11 were in the *Saracen*. X11 itself, with her caretaker crew of three, was towed behind us on a long cable. Each X-craft had been trimmed down at the bows so that it trailed about 40 feet below the depth of her parent-submarine. In this way it was hoped that any enemy planes that spotted the larger subs wouldn't spot the midget ones also.

As we travelled in the relative comfort of the *Saracen* I thought with sympathy of the caretaker crews on board the X-crafts. While the parent-subs travelled on the surface at night, the midgets had to keep submerged, only coming up every six hours or so to change the air.

It's a strange life, being in a submarine. All the things you take for granted on land become amazingly precious. Like air. The only oxygen in a submarine is the stuff that's there before you close the hatch. Once they're shut, you begin to breathe less and less oxygen and more and more carbon dioxide. The longer you stay below the surface, the greater the percentage of carbon dioxide you take in. For that reason, most submarines remain on the surface as long as they can, only diving when necessary.

If the worst happens and the sub sinks and you can't get out, then all you breathe is carbon dioxide and you eventually die of suffocation.

Fresh water is also very limited in a submarine. The first thing to go is washing. Not that it matters, because if no one in the crew washes, then after a while no one notices the smell of body odour. One sure way to disguise it is never to take your clothes off. So most of us submariners, when out on patrol, kept the same clothes on all the time, often for weeks on end. After a long patrol, whenever I arrive home for shore leave and finally take my clothes off, a layer of white powder falls off my body. Dead skin!

Going to the toilet is another problem in a submarine. There are toilets, but often they don't work, and more than one submariner I know has suffered the embarrassment of flushing a toilet under water and being covered by the contents as they came back under pressure. As a result, most submariners prefer to use a bucket, which is then emptied out when the hatch is opened. The inside of a submarine that has been under water for a long time is not a great place for someone with a delicate sense of smell.

*

On our second day out I was called to see Commander Perry, the commander of the *Saracen* and the leader of this small flotilla of submarines.

'Well, lieutenant, it's time to co-ordinate the rest of the operation,' Perry told me. 'Your orders once you've left us.' He opened a buff envelope and took out a sheet of paper. 'At this same moment, the commanders of the other submarines in this flotilla are issuing these same orders to your fellow X-craft officers.' He handed me the sheet of paper. It simply said: 'T-time will be 0800 hours after embarkation. Rendezvous for return twelve hours later, at 2000 hours.'

'Thank you, sir,' I said, handing it back to him.

I returned to the cramped and tiny quarters I shared with my fellow crewmen from X11 and filled them in on the instructions I'd just received.

'T-time is at 0800 after we leave the *Saracen*,' I told them.

'Eight o'clock in the morning is break-fast-time, not tea-time,' pointed out Stevens.

'Target-time, idiot,' grumbled Munro, but

not with any spite. To my relief, he'd become quite used to Stevens' jokey manner in the time we'd spent together.

'I know that,' grinned Stevens. 'You know your trouble, Scotty? You wouldn't know a joke if it came up to you and bit you on the ankle.'

'All the other crews are getting the same instructions, so if we're not away from the *Tirpitz* by eight o'clock on the morning of Target Day, we'll be among the casualties on the bottom of a Norwegian fjord.'

'And getting back?' asked Stevens.

'2000 hours, twelve hours later,' I said. 'If we miss that, we miss the bus home.'

We had been at sea for four days when we ran into trouble. We were on the surface, hatches open, along with the other four subs. Each, as usual, was towing its midget behind, beneath the surface. Today we were at the head of the flotilla.

I was standing in the conning-tower along with Commander Perry, both of us rolling slightly with the movement of the sub as it ploughed through the North Atlantic waves. We were scanning the sea ahead through binoculars. Suddenly I glimpsed something on the horizon.

'Possible enemy due east, sir!' I said.

Commander Perry was already looking through his glasses.

'Well spotted, lieutenant!'

There was no doubt about it: a wolf-pack of German U-boats, running on the surface, just like us. I counted six conning-towers.

Commander Perry scrambled down the ladder into the hull of the sub. I followed him and heard him give the order to close the hatch.

'Alert the others,' Perry ordered his wireless operator. 'Wolf-pack on the horizon.'

The crew moved to their stations, getting ready for action.

'Where do you want me and my men, sir?' I asked Perry.

'You stay with me, lieutenant, in case I need you,' said Perry. 'Assign your crew for'ard with the torpedo operators.'

I hurried to our quarters to let Stevens, Munro and Watson know the situation. As I did, I squeezed past the wireless operator and heard him reporting the situation to the rest of our small fleet.

'Enemy wolf-pack approaching from east. Position latitude sixty-three degrees, three degrees longitude. Six in number. All boats to action stations.'

Stevens, Munro and Watson were all ready for action.

'What's happening, skipper?' asked Stevens.

'It looks like we're in for a fight,' I said. 'The commander would rather avoid it and get us to Norway, but I don't think this lot are going to miss the opportunity for a scrap. Especially when they've got a one-sub advantage.'

'Where does the commander want us?' asked Watson.

'Helping the torpedo operators,' I replied.

'Suits me,' said Munro. 'Anything I can do to sink a few U-boats, count me in.'

My three crewmen hurried forward to the torpedo tubes, while I returned to midships. Commander Perry was standing with the radar operator, watching the sonar of the approaching U-boats on the screen. It was hazy, but the blips were there all right, as were the other blips indicating our own subs. They had joined us now and we were strung out in a line, heading towards the six U-boats.

The initial noise of the submarine crew swinging into action had died down. Everyone was at their positions, waiting. The only sounds were the bleeps from the sonar and the occasional crackle from the wireless as the subs communicated with each other, updating enemy positions.

'Set torpedo one for two and a half miles,' Commander Perry said into the communication tube.

From the for'ard compartment we heard the clanking of a torpedo being loaded into number one tube, ready for firing.

'Range?' asked the commander.

'Three and a half miles and closing,' said the sonar operator. 'Three and a quarter. Three miles. Two and three-quarters –'

'Ready –' Perry ordered.

'Two and a half –'

'Fire!'

There was a hiss and our submarine recoiled in the water as a torpedo was discharged.

'Incoming enemy torpedo!' came a warning shout from the sonar operator.

Chapter 7
Sunk

'Alter course!' shouted Perry. 'Bearing five nine zero.'

The command was passed along inside the hull. I felt the *Saracen* lurch as it turned sharply to port, then straighten on to an even keel, still heading for the U-boats. On the sonar screen we saw the German torpedo heading in our direction, but on a bearing that would take it past us.

The sonar showed that the leading U-boat had swung away slightly to avoid our torpedo, and the rest of the wolf-pack had followed it. We were now almost level with the U-boats.

'Hard to port.' ordered Perry, and the shout went down the lines of communication. 'Hard to port.'

The metal hull of the *Saracen* creaked under pressure as the engines were thrown into reverse and the flaps raised to bring us sharply round. The other four subs in our group had also begun to fan out so that all five of us moved behind the U-boats.

On the sonar we watched the German wolf-pack separate and begin to turn.

The commander smiled grimly.

'Right,' he said. 'Lay two torpedoes ahead of the target in the eastern sector. Fire on my mark.'

The inside of the submarine fell almost silent. The only sounds were the metal on metal of the two torpedoes being loaded into the tubes, and the bleep of the sonar.

We studied the sonar screen, watching our target turn away from the rest of the wolf-pack. The Germans were obviously intent on picking us off one by one.

'Steady,' called Perry, and the *Saracen* shuddered, the metal of the hull creaking as we slowed. 'Bearing five three seven.'

We altered direction slightly, on to a collision course with our target.

'Fire!' shouted Perry.

The *Saracen* rocked violently in the water as the two torpedoes rocketed from their tubes. The torpedoes clear, Perry ordered another shift in our course to take us away from our target.

On the sonar I spotted one of the U-boats moving into a position where it would be able to hit us.

'Sir!' I called.

Perry had already spotted it.

'Hard about,' he said crisply.

'Hard about it is, sir,' came the response.

Again the *Saracen* shuddered in the water, kicking against the abrupt change of forward motion. I dreaded to think what all this was doing to the crew in the X11. With no communications and given their size, the craft would be taking a terrible battering.

There was a sudden deafening noise as our torpedoes hit their target, blowing it up. There was no time for celebrations, however, because we were too busy trying to get away from the firing line of the other German subs.

Perry's order of 'Hard about' was just in time: another U-boat had fired its torpedoes straight at our forward position. All of us heard the terrifying sound of German torpedoes in the water, echoing inside the sub. We waited, motionless, holding our breath as the *Saracen* desperately banked, continuing its turn. There was a loud *WOOOSH* as the torpedoes just missed us.

We were overwhelmed by the sounds of explosions as torpedoes from the other vessels hit, though whether it was our torpedoes hitting the U-boats or German torpedoes hitting our subs, we couldn't tell.

I tried to get a better idea of the situation from the sonar screen, but the noise had scrambled everything, fuzzing the screen. Then I saw movement: four blips heading away north.

Commander Perry rapped out an order to the wireless operator: 'Regroup ten degrees south-south-east. Alert rest of flotilla.'

'Regroup ten degrees south-south-east,' repeated the wireless operator. 'Copy?'

Back came the replies from the other submarines.

'Copy, *Snug*.'

'Copy, *Scavenger.*'

'Copy, *Siskin.*'

I waited for the fifth and final signal: 'Copy, *Sealy.*' *Sealy* was the sub that was carrying Peter Redford and the crew of X5. There was silence amid the bubbling sounds of the sea outside.

The wireless operator looked questioningly at Commander Perry.

'Send out a signal to *Sealy* asking for confirmation,' said Perry.

'*Saracen* to *Sealy*, did you receive last message?' the wireless operator said into his microphone.

There was no response.

'*Saracen* to *Sealy*,' repeated the wireless operator. 'Come in, please.'

I looked at the sonar. The four blips that indicated the surviving German U-boats were now nearly off the screen as they made their escape. That left just four blips on the screen, grouped together: *Saracen*, *Snug*, *Scavenger* and *Siskin*. *Sealy* had vanished.

Chapter 8
Norway

We continued our journey in a sombre mood. Four of the U-boats had made their getaway, leaving two of their number on the bottom. Our losses had been the fewer, just the *Sealy* and the X5 midget sub. But we'd all lost good friends and we felt the emptiness of their loss. It was especially hard for me. I couldn't believe Peter Redford was dead. My best friend . . .

Once we were sure the Germans were out of range, our four surviving subs surfaced and with each sub's commander in their conning towers, Commander Perry conducted a short service for our fallen comrades, saying just a few words to commend their bodies to the deep. Then we set sail again, making our way across the turbulent seas of the North Atlantic towards Norway.

Although we'd lost one of the X-craft the mission would still go ahead, but now with only four of us making the *Tirpitz* our target instead of five.

For the next three days we proceeded in convoy, staying on the surface where possible, diving when danger threatened. We couldn't afford another battle in which more of the precious X-crafts might be lost.

As we cruised just beneath the waves, one of the submarine commanders would spot a German tanker or a supply ship. Under normal circumstances we would have attacked and sunk it, but Commander Perry had been given express orders that our mission was too important to be jeopardized by an unnecessary encounter that could bring us to the enemy's attention.

On the eighth day we reached Norwegian territorial waters. Perhaps it would have been more accurate to call them 'German-controlled Norwegian territorial waters', since the Nazis had invaded and taken control of Norway.

I was sitting in our quarters playing cards with Stevens, Munro and Watson, when a young rating arrived and interrupted our game.

'Lieutenant Smith,' he said. 'Compliments of the commander, he needs to see you right away.'

I looked down at the hand I was holding: four aces and the king of hearts. It was the first decent hand I'd been dealt in two hours of playing.

'When the commander says right away . . .?' I queried, tempted to delay my departure until this hand had been played.

'He means *right away*, sir,' said the rating. With that, he disappeared.

Stevens saw the look on my face and grinned. 'If I was a betting man, which I'm not, I'd say you had a hand that was sure to win this game, whatever any of us is holding.'

'And you could be right,' I said ruefully, throwing my cards down on the box top we were using as a card table and getting up.

It was Munro who picked up my fallen cards as I left the tiny room. I heard him laugh out loud and reflected that at least I'd cheered that usually unhappy Scot up and given him something to laugh about.

Commander Perry was waiting for me by the periscope. He stepped away from it as I approached.

'Take a look,' he said.

I put my eyes to the periscope. In front of me was a rugged coastline, a forbidding landscape of bleak high mountains.

'The Norwegian coast,' announced Perry as I moved away from the periscope. 'We've arrived. Time to transfer you to your X-craft.'

We surfaced out of range of any coastal watchers. Then began the task of changing crews. We sent a rubber dinghy over from the *Sarocen* to the X11. The caretaker crew slid down from the deck of the tiny sub into it. Their relief at being out of the cramped craft was obvious. All three men looked pale. In fact, it seemed to me, as we helped them on board the *Saracen*, that there was a bluey-green tinge to the sickly white pallor of their skin. Whether it was the high levels of carbon dioxide in the midget sub, or the rough crossing, I didn't have time to ask. Stevens, Munro, Watson and I were too busy getting ready for the return trip back to X11. Just before I stepped down into the dinghy, Commander Perry stopped me.

'Officially your orders tell you to rendezvous here at 2000 hours tomorrow evening,' he said. 'However, German patrols permitting, we'll try to give you a few hours' grace. I'm sure that, if you manage to sink the *Tirpitz*, the Admiralty will have the decency to allow you that extra time. But we can't stay here indefinitely. After 2200 hours we will have to head for home.'

I nodded. 'Understood, sir.'

Then I joined the other three in the dinghy and we set out for our midget sub.

The inside of X11 seemed even smaller than I remembered it. It was also swimming with small pools of stagnant water.

'It stinks!' exclaimed Stevens.

'We're only going to be in this thing for just over twenty-four hours,' I pointed out. 'The poor blighters who've just left it spent eight days in here.'

'Yeah, but I bet it didn't smell like this for the first few days,' replied Watson.

We squashed into our places and made last-minute checks of the equipment. Everything seemed to be in working order. The caretaker crew had done a good job of maintaining her on the rough journey over.

I climbed the short ladder and took a last look out through the open hatch at the large subs that had brought us here, at the open sea and at the Norwegian coast. The commanders of X6, X7 and X8 were doing the same thing. We saluted each other and then prepared to dive. I dropped back down the ladder and pulled the hatch shut.

'Take us down, engineer,' I said.

'Aye, aye, sir,' said Munro.

The air hissed out of our tanks as ballast water filled them and we began to submerge. We were now out of contact with all other human beings. Ahead of us were the icy waters of the channels that led to the fjords, floating mines, anti-submarine nets, batteries of German guns . . . and the mighty *Tirpitz*.

'S' Class

Specification
Standard surface displacement: 715 tons (726 tonnes)
Overall length: 217 ft (66.14 m)
Maximum beam: 23 ft 9 in (7.13 m)
Surface speed: 14.5 knots
Underwater speed: 10 knots
Range at 10 knots: 6,000 miles (9,656 km)
Torpedo tubes: 6 bow, 1 stern
Reload torpedoes: 6
Guns: 1 x 3 in; 1 x 20 mm anti-aircraft
Diving depth: 300 — 350 ft (91 — 107 m)
Crew: 44

The original 'S' Class subs in the early 1930s had
six bow torpedo tubes with six reload torpedoes.
They were designed for patrol work in the North
Sea. Their standard surface displacement was 670
tons (681 tonnes). After the outbreak of World War
Two a new 'S' Class was produced, heavier at 715
tons (726 tonnes), and with the addition of a single
torpedo tube at the stern. The 'S' Class subs,
however, were slow when compared with the German
submarines, having a surface speed of just 14 knots
against the faster U-boats' 29 knots.

'T' Class

Specification

Standard surface displacement: 1,090 tons (1,107 tonnes)
Overall length: 275 ft (83.82 m)
Maximum beam: 26 ft 7 in (8.1 m)
Surface speed: 15.25 knots
Underwater speed: 8.5 knots
Range at 10 knots: 8,000 miles (12,874 km)
Torpedo tubes: 10 bow (later versions: 8 bow, 3 stern)
Reload torpedoes: 6
Guns: 1 x 4 in; 1 x 20 mm anti-aircraft
Diving depth: 300 ft (91.44 m)
Crew: 46 — 61

The 'T' Class submarine was built to replace the 'O'
and 'P' Classes, which had suffered many technical
problems, most notably a tendency to leak oil from
their external tanks. The 'T' Class subs had one major
advantage over their predecessors: a bow salvo of ten
torpedoes. Six tubes opened from the forward end of
the pressure hull, two from the casing above, and a
further two faced forward under a raised deck at mid-
length. Only fifty 'T' Class subs were built, as they
proved to be very slow in the water.

'U' Class

Specification
Standard surface displacement: 540 tons (549 tonnes)
Overall length: 197 ft (60 m)
Maximum beam: 16 ft (4.88 m)
Surface speed: 11.25 knots
Underwater speed: 9 knots
Range at 10 knots: 3,800 miles (6,093 km)
Torpedo tubes: 4 bow
Reload torpedoes: 4
Guns: 1 x 3 in
Diving depth: 200 ft (60.96 m)
Crew: 31

'U' Class subs were originally designed as unarmed boats to train surface forces in anti-submarine action. With the approach of war, they were equipped with four internal and two external bow torpedo tubes. Unfortunately, the bulbous casing needed for these additions led to problems: when a full salvo was fired the boat invariably surfaced. As a result, after trials with the first three modified boats, the external tubes were omitted.

X-craft

Specification
Standard surface displacement: 30 tons (30.48 tonnes)
Overall length: 51 ft (15.55 m)
Maximum beam: 5 ft 6 in (1.68 m)
Surface speed: 6 knots
Underwater speed: 5 knots
Crew: 4

The X-craft were based on a prototype developed privately by a retired submariner, Commander Cromwell Varley, on the Hamble River in Hampshire. They were submarines in miniature, but without conning-tower or torpedo tubes. Instead they had side-cargoes that contained time-fused high-explosive charges. They were very cramped indeed. Unlike the faster (although slightly larger) Japanese 'A' Type midget submarines, the X-craft had a diesel engine for surface cruising and recharging batteries, and an electric motor for submerged running.

German submarines

U-boat Type VIIA

Specification
Standard surface displacement: 500 tons (508 tonnes)
Overall length: 206 ft 9 in (63 m)
Maximum beam: 19 ft 4 in (5.89 m)
Surface speed: 16.5 knots
Underwater speed: 8 knots
Torpedo tubes: 4 bow, 1 stern
Guns: 1 x 3.5 in; 1 x 1 pdr
Crew: 35

U35 was built by Germania and was launched on 29
September 1936. During that year at least nine U-
boats were built to a similar specification.

U-boat Type VIIB

Specification
Standard surface displacement: 517 tons (525 tonnes)
Overall length: 213 ft 3 in (65 m)
Maximum beam: 19 ft 4 in (5.89 m)
Surface speed: 16.5 knots
Underwater speed: 8 knots
Torpedo tubes: 4 bow, 1 stern
Guns: 1 x 3.2 in ; 1 x 1 pdr
Crew: 35

U45 was commissioned on 25 June 1938 and was built by Germania. U46 was launched later that year on 2 November and U47 on 7 December.

U-boat Type V11C

Specification
Standard surface displacement: 760 tons (772 tonnes)
Overall length: 220 ft 2 in (67.1 m)
Maximum beam: 20 ft 4 in (6.2 m)
Surface speed: 17 knots
Underwater speed: 7.5 knots
Range at 10 knots: 8,500 miles (13,679 km)
Torpedo tubes: 4 bow, 1 stern
Reload torpedoes: 9
Guns: 1 x 3.5 in; 2 x 20 mm
Diving depth: 400 ft (122 m)
Crew: 44

The VII was one of two German submarines based on
the World War One U-boat (the other was the smaller
Type II at 250 tons/254 tonnes). The major
modification of both of these new U-boats over the
original was the reduction in the size of the
conning-tower to reduce the silhouette on the
surface. The Type VII was not intended for direct
battle but for blockading action against warships.
The Type VII played a major part in the Battle of
the Atlantic against Allied merchant shipping.

The *Tirpitz*

Specification
Displacement: 42,900 tons (43,586 tonnes)
Overall length: 791 ft (241 m)
Overall breadth: 118 ft 3 in (36 m)
Speed: 29 knots
Armament:
        8 x 15 in (4 x 2) guns
        12 x 5.9 in guns
        16 x 4.1 in anti-aircraft guns
        16 x 37 mm anti-aircraft guns
        16 x 20 mm anti-aircraft guns
        48 x machine guns
        8 x 21 torpedo tubes
        4 aircraft
Crew: 1,500 (of which 103 were officers, including
ship's surgeons and midshipmen)

Along with its sister ship, *Bismarck*, the *Tirpitz* was
one of the two giant battleships of the German Navy.
In January 1942 she sailed from Wilhlemshaven to
Norway, where she spent her entire career. In fact,
Tirpitz never took part in any actual surface
action, but instead stayed securely in the Norwegian
fjords as a constant threat to the Allied Arctic
convoys.

Chapter 9

Through the Minefield

According to our information, the *Tirpitz* was in the safe harbour of Kaafjord, at the head of Altenfjord, twelve miles inland from the open sea. Various obstacles lay ahead of us before we could even get into Kaafjord itself. The first were the German minefields. Although they were anchored in certain areas of the fjord so as not to present a hazard to German shipping, we didn't know their exact location. They posed a serious threat to us.

The second problem was the amount of sea traffic passing up and down the long Altenfjord. Any one of these vessels might spot us and relay information about our position to the German look-out posts, which were armed with heavy guns and depth-charges.

If we got past those hazards, then we would come up against the boom across the entrance to Kaafjord. This was like a level-crossing gate – a long arm across the entrance to the inner fjord which was raised and lowered by the guards on the quay. Beneath it hung a metal net to prevent submarines getting in.

If we managed to get past that, then the next obstacle was the chainmail-like anti-torpedo net surrounding the *Tirpitz*, suspended from floating buoys. If we got tangled up in it, we'd be well and truly trapped.

Finally there were *Tirpitz*'s own defences: heavy and light guns, depth-charges, backed up with sharp-eyed look-outs and sonar devices.

The sea-bed itself also presented a danger since the depth of water constantly changed. If we ran aground in the silt and shingle we could damage our craft. At worst we could get stuck on the bottom and have to abandon ship, swimming out through the Wet and Dry room. For all of us on board X11 that was not an option because of the danger of being spotted. We couldn't afford to alert the Germans that an attack on the *Tirpitz* was taking place and foul things up for the others. So, if we got stuck on the sea-bed, we'd have to stay put until we heard an explosion to tell us that one of the other X-crafts had been successful.

Our main problem in getting past all these obstacles was that we were trying to do it with limited instruments. Our only navigational aids were the periscope, compass and a constant check on our speed to help us estimate the distance we'd travelled. The rest, including our position in the fjord, was based on guesswork and keeping our senses alert. With no wireless, we also had no way of knowing how the other X-crafts were doing.

We kept to fifty feet, making four knots, listening out for other vessels.

'Was it like this before?' I asked Munro. 'When you were here with the Chariots?'

Munro gave a bitter laugh. 'The nearest we got before was landing on the Norwegian coast. We lost the Chariots before we got to the fjord.'

'What happened?' asked Watson.

And so, as we cruised quietly along the long Altenfjord, Munro told his tale.

'There were four of us. Two men to each Chariot. We were on a Norwegian fishing boat, disguised as fishermen. The two Chariots were bolted to the bottom of the fishing boat, which slowed us down on our journey across the Atlantic.'

'You were lucky you weren't spotted by a German patrol,' said Stevens.

'We were spotted,' said Munro. 'They picked us up in Norwegian waters. Luckily for us our captain, a very brave Norwegian, persuaded them that we were just honest fishermen on our way back to port with fish for the brave German protectors.

'After that incident we thought we were home and dry. We'd made it across fifteen hundred miles of freezing, rough seas, talked our way past a German patrol; all we had to do was disconnect the Chariots and get into Trondheim fjord, and that would be it. Bang would go the *Tirpitz*.'

'What went wrong?' I asked.

'The bolts holding the Chariots to the bottom of the trawler failed,' said Munro. 'We lost the Chariots. Both of them. They came loose and sank right down to the bottom into a trench, too deep for us to recover them.' He shrugged. 'That was it. Mission abandoned. We daren't take a chance on going back on the same trawler, and getting picked up, so the captain put us ashore and we made our way on foot across the mountains to Sweden.'

Munro fell silent for a moment, then continued, 'The Germans caught up with us. Ambushed us. Robbie, my brother, got shot. The rest of us managed to get away, into Sweden. And the Swedes got us back home.'

Munro's story had an effect on all of us. We felt for him. To have got all that way, and to fail because of something as silly as some faulty bolts. Even Stevens didn't want to make a joke about it.

All the time Munro had been talking I was keeping a close watch through the periscope. As he finished, I suddenly saw something in the dark waters ahead. There were cables stretching up from the bed of the fjord. Mines!

'Slow ahead, group down,' I ordered.

'Slow ahead, group down, sir,' came the response from Munro.

'What is it, skipper?' asked Watson.

'A minefield. We must be getting near to the entrance to Kaafjord.'

Above us were German mines. Through the water I could see their spines reaching down towards us. One touch of our hull on the end of those metal probes and we'd be blown sky-high.

I gave instructions and slowly, very slowly, Stevens steered us first to the right, then to the left as we wormed our way through the forest of metal cables. Only a midget submarine could have manoeuvred through them, anything larger would have snagged a cable, pulled the mine down and *BOOM*.

After what seemed an eternity we cleared the last cable. We had done it – we were out of the minefield.

I checked my watch: 0300 hours. Five hours to go before we were due to sink the *Tirpitz*. All the manoeuvring to get through the minefield had made distance-judging difficult, but according to my calculations I guessed that we were approaching the boom that separated Altenfjord from Kaafjord.

'Periscope depth,' I ordered.

'Periscope depth it is, sir.'

Slowly we came up from our cruising depth of fifty feet.

'Stop motor,' I said.

'Stop motor.'

I looked through the periscope. In the early morning light I could just make out the boom across the entrance to Kaafjord. My calculations had been correct.

'How's it look, skipper?' asked Watson.

'Looking good so far,' I said. Then a movement on the surface caught my eye and I turned the periscope slightly to the right to get a better view. It was a small coaster heading towards the entrance to Kaafjord. As I watched I saw the boom begin to rise, the wire netting beginning to emerge from the water.

'They're lifting the boom!'

'What!' said Munro, surprised.

'They're letting a coaster through. Right,

let's see if we can slip in on its wake. Start motor. Full speed ahead. Take us down to just below periscope depth.'

Munro opened the vents while Stevens set a course for the boom. All of us felt frustrated by the X-craft's slow speed. Would we make it before the Germans brought the boom down? Had the other X-crafts spotted the boom going up? Were they behind us? Was one of them already inside Kaafjord? There were so many questions and no way of knowing the answers. We were putting everything we could into willing X11 to go faster.

'Speed?' I snapped impatiently.

'Five knots,' replied Stevens.

'Can't you push it any faster? If we don't get to the entrance soon, that boom will be down. And if we get caught in that wire netting –'

'Increasing speed,' said Stevens. 'Five and a quarter knots . . . five and a half . . .'

Already we could hear the metal of the X-craft groaning as Stevens pushed it faster, the engines starting to squeal in protest at being made to work harder than they were designed to. Six knots was possible on the surface, but against the pressure of the water . . .

'She won't last, skipper,' warned Munro urgently.

'OK, reduce speed,' I ordered reluctantly. 'But keep it as fast as you –'

My words were cut off as a scraping sound echoed throughout the sub. The metal of the boom's netting. They'd lowered the boom.

'Slow ahead, group down!' I yelled sharply. 'Dead stop. Dive dive dive!'

The last thing we wanted was to get our propellers tangled up in the wire of the boom.

Munro and Stevens worked together, bringing X11 to a shuddering stop and sending her down until we felt her scrape the bottom of the fjord.

'Stop motor,' I instructed.

With the motor cut off, we listened. Metal on metal. There was no doubt about it, we were caught in the boom's net.

Chapter 10
Tragedy

'OK, Watson,' I said, 'you're on. Get us out of this.'

'On my way, skipper.'

With Munro's help Watson pulled on his bulky diver's suit – a real struggle in the confines of the midget submarine. Then he pulled on his flippers, picked up his oxygen mask and goggles, and finally the huge pair of wire cutters.

Stevens opened the door to the Wet and Dry room and Watson hauled himself into the tiny cramped space. He then spun the huge wheel, sealing the door shut.

'All ready, skipper.'

'Shut number two main vent,' I instructed.

'Number two main vent shut,' nodded

Munro as he opened the tanks to flood the W & D room.

'Shut number two Kingston.'

'Number two Kingston shut,' said Munro as he turned the second valve.

We could see the water level rising through the tiny porthole in the door. Watson gave us a thumbs-up sign as the water covered him. Then we heard the outside hatch open.

From my seat in the command position, I looked through the viewing port above me and saw Watson swim out of the hatch, grab hold of the thick wire netting and start to cut through it.

When Watson had cut a big enough hole for us to get free, he swam back in through the hatch. We heard the outer hatch shut, then a knock from inside the W & D room. Watson's hand appeared in the porthole, thumb raised.

'Open number two main vent,' I ordered. 'Open number two Kingston.'

As before, Munro repeated each command as he opened the valves to drain the W & D room.

With the water gone, Munro spun the

wheel to open the hatch and Watson scrambled back inside.

'I think there's enough room to get clear if we edge forward slowly, skipper,' he said.

'Let's hope so. OK, Stevens, start the motor. Slow ahead, group down.'

Watson had done a good job. We moved forward, each movement brushing clear of the tangles of wire from the boom net.

'Right,' I said. 'We've made it into Kaafjord. Next stop, *Tirpitz*.'

I waited until I reckoned we were well past the boom before giving the order to come up to just beneath the surface.

'Blow tube.'

'Tube blown, sir.'

I hoped that here, in the middle of the wide fjord, a tiny object such as our periscope top wouldn't be noticed by the shore batteries and that the guards' attention would be concentrated out towards Altenfjord rather than inside the boom.

I looked through the periscope, and there she was! About three miles away. The *Tirpitz*. Even from this distance she looked gigantic. Suddenly there was a flicker of movement at the edge of the periscope lens. I turned towards it and I was confronted by the terrifying sight of a ship's bows bearing down on us at speed.

'*Crash dive! Dive dive dive!*' I shouted urgently.

Munro and Stevens worked furiously, opening the ballast tanks and altering course. As we went down we heard the hiss of air bubbles rush past outside and we were thrown about violently, the hull creaking ominously. We clearly heard the whine of propellers as the ship sailed over-head, missing us by what must have been barely inches.

'Phew!' said Watson, wiping the sweat from his forehead. 'That was a close one. Must've been a supply ship.'

'Let's hope *Tirpitz* has got everything she wants for the next few hours,' I said. 'I don't fancy coming that close again.'

I checked my watch: 0530 hours. Just two and a half hours to target-time. I wondered how the other X-crafts were getting on.

'Slow speed ahead,' I ordered.

'Slow speed ahead,' nodded Stevens.

From here, according to the charts, the sea-bed began to rise. The last thing I wanted was to scrape along the bottom and run aground, so slow ahead was the rule of the moment.

There was also the problem of the anti-torpedo nets surrounding the *Tirpitz* – another reason for proceeding cautiously; I didn't relish hitting them full on, even at just five knots.

'Steady as we go,' I murmured.

'Steady as we go, sir,' repeated Stevens.

Suddenly we heard the sound of an explosion rumbling through the water. But it didn't come from ahead of us, from the *Tirpitz*. It came from behind. We exchanged glances.

'It came from the other side of the boom, sir,' said Munro. 'From Altenfjord . . .'

'And that was more than just depth-charges,' muttered Watson angrily.

I nodded. The noise and the shock waves from the explosion, even at this distance, meant that the charges of one of the other X-crafts had blown up. Four tons of explosives. One of our subs had gone down, and with it four of our comrades. I wondered which one it was. And what had caused it. Had the Germans spotted it and fired at it or depth-charged it, causing its bombs to go off?

'They'll be looking for us now, sir,' said Munro.

'Then we'd better get on and blow up the *Tirpitz* before they find us,' I said grimly.

Chapter 11

Caught in the Nets

As the after-shocks of the massive explosion in Altenfjord died away behind us, we moved slowly forward through the water of Kaafjord on course for the *Tirpitz*. We were aware that from now on the gunners on the massive German battleship would be watching out for any signs of enemy encroachment. Surfacing was out of the question. We had to inch along the bottom of the fjord, trying to avoid rocks, floating mines, anything that could damage our craft.

I kept my fingers crossed that the Germans would think the craft that had been destroyed in Altenfjord was the leader of the fleet and so concentrate their search for other vessels in the outer fjord. If they did that, I could also only hope that the remaining two X-crafts had made it through into Kaafjord.

'Still steady as we go, sir,' whispered Stevens.

'Keep it that way,' I murmured back.

We had to talk quietly now in case the Germans were listening with hydrophones.

'I calculate we should be nearing the anti-torpedo net now, sir,' whispered Munro.

I kept my eyes pressed against the eye-piece of the periscope.

'Got it,' I said.

I could see dimly through the water the small-meshed metal net hanging like a curtain in front of us.

'Slow ahead, group down,' I ordered.

'Slow ahead, group down,' repeated Stevens.

'Stop motor.' The less noise going through the water that might give away our position, the better.

Through the periscope I could see that there was a gap of about four feet between the base of the net and the bed of the fjord. Too low for us to go through without getting snared in the net. Cutting through a net with such a small mesh would lose us too much time. We also had to be careful not to move the net in case we disturbed the buoys floating on the surface. The look-outs on the *Tirpitz* would be scanning the surface waters of the fjord and any sudden bobbing about by the buoys that held the anti-torpedo nets would alert the lookouts to our presence and lead to a major attack on us. Stealth was the only way to get our two charges to the *Tirpitz*.

'OK, Watson,' I said quietly. 'Time for you to go back into action. There is a chance that we can scrape through, but we need another two feet above us to get clearance without drawing attention to ourselves. Cut a line about a foot up from the bottom of the net. Then I want you to see if you can lift it long enough for us to slide under.'

'I'll do my best, skipper.'

Once again he pulled on his thick rubber suit, oxygen mask and flippers. Then, taking his cutters with him, he crawled into the W & D room and we went through the procedure to flood it so that he could swim out.

As before, through the tiny porthole we watched the W & D room fill with water, then the hatch opened, and I turned my full attention to the periscope eye-piece and watched Watson swim out towards the anti-torpedo net.

Watson swam to the bottom of the net and began to cut. The work was harder this time because of the smaller mesh. It was also much slower, because the buoys had to remain undisturbed on the surface. The tension inside X11 as we waited was almost unbelievable. In the silence I could hear the blood pounding in my head.

Three inches. Four. Five. Carefully, painstakingly, Watson cut upwards. Six inches. Seven. Eight.

I could feel Munro's and Stevens' eyes on me as I watched Watson through the periscope. They were waiting for me to tell them what was going on and whether Watson was succeeding.

'Nearly there,' I whispered to them.

Nine inches. Ten. Eleven. Watson made one final cut to give me the twelve-inch line

I'd requested. He turned towards the periscope and gave me a thumbs-up.

'Start up motor,' I ordered quietly.

The motor hummed into life.

'Right, dead slow ahead. And I do mean *dead slow*. I want us just to slide through. But if we do get caught, I want to be able to stop at once. I don't want to pull the net along with us and drag down the buoys.'

'Dead slow it is, sir,' said Stevens. The craft moved forward very slowly.

'Keep her down,' I ordered Munro. 'Scrape the bottom if necessary, but keep her down as low as she'll go.'

'Keeping her low, sir,' nodded Munro.

Through the periscope I saw Watson grab hold of the anti-torpedo net and swim upwards, lifting it with him. I knew he daren't take it up much because of the risk of surface disturbance, but I had calculated that all we needed was that extra foot and we could hopefully slide through under it.

'Steady as she goes.'

As we moved forward, Watson floated into view through the viewing port above me. We were now underneath him. There was a scraping sound as the net brushed against our hull.

'Still steady ahead,' I murmured.

I could feel myself sweating. I'd taken us beyond the point of no return. We were at that crucial point where the net was draped on top of us. If we attempted to reverse now, we'd get snared up. From beneath us there was an ominous groaning and a grating sound.

'Hull's on the bottom, sir,' reported Munro. 'Take her up?' Beads of sweat stood out on his face.

If I took her up I was sure we'd get tangled in the net. If I didn't, there was a good chance that we'd damage ourselves on the rock beds of the fjord or we could run aground on the shingle. My decision now really would mean life or death.

Chapter 12

Bombs Away

I made up my mind. 'We're staying down. Keep her steady. Let's hope Watson can hold that net up high enough for us to sneak under.'

Slowly, ever so slowly, we moved forward, inch by inch. At any second I expected us to lurch to a sudden halt as we snagged on either the net or the sea-bed, but we continued to slide slowly forward. Then the net scraping on our hull ceased. We had made it.

'OK, take us up three feet,' I ordered. 'No more.'

'Decreasing depth by three feet,' said Munro.

Meanwhile Watson had returned.

'That was a tight one!' he gasped. 'I don't

know how we're going to get under going back.'

'One step at a time,' I said. 'First, we have to deal with the *Tirpitz*.'

I looked at my watch. 0710. Fifty minutes to T-time.

'Did you see any sign of the others while you were out there, Watson?' I asked.

'I'm not sure, sir,' said Watson. 'The water's fairly thick with all the silt that has been churned up from the bottom. I think I saw something that could have been one of ours, but I didn't want to swim over and investigate in case it wasn't.'

'Did you get a look at the *Tirpitz*?' I asked.

'Two hundreds yards to starboard. You can't miss her. Her hull is nearly touching the bottom of the fjord.'

'Good,' I said. 'Let's get there and drop our load.'

I went to the periscope, at the same time ordering Stevens to change course forty degrees to starboard. We came about and there she was. Even through the murky waters there was no mistaking her.

'OK, take us in, dead ahead. And steady

as she goes. We don't want to crash into her, not with four tons of explosives on board. They may sink the *Tirpitz*, but I'd rather we didn't go down with her.'

As we moved slowly towards the hull of the giant German battleship, I couldn't help but think of our comrades who hadn't made it, blown up just a couple of hours ago, so near to their target, yet so far. I was determined we would succeed, if only for them. We were now almost beneath the enormous hull.

'Arm cargoes,' I ordered. 'Set for forty minutes.'

Munro set the timers on both of our two-ton explosive charges. 'Cargoes armed, sir.'

'Drop cargoes.'

We heard a very dull thud as the two huge bombs rolled out on to the bottom of the fjord.

'Cargo one away, sir,' reported Munro.

'Cargo two away, sir,' echoed Stevens.

'Right,' I said, 'We've got just over thirty-five minutes before they go off. Let's get out of here!'

As we turned, I glimpsed through the

periscope something in the water about 200 yards away, further along *Tirpitz*'s hull. It was another X-craft!

I grinned broadly and told the others, 'We're not alone, boys. Someone else has got through. I guess they've just managed to drop their charges as well. That means there are now at least eight tons due to go off. We'd better take a chance and put some distance between us and the explosion. Full speed ahead.'

'Full speed ahead it is, sir,' responded Stevens enthusiastically.

I kept a close eye on my watch all the way back to the anti-torpedo net, watching the minutes tick away. When I saw the net ahead I gave the order, 'Slow ahead, group down.'

'Slow ahead, group down, sir,' repeated Munro.

The X-craft slowed in the water and then came to rest, with its nose touching the net.

'Right, Watson,' I said, 'out you go again. Lift that thing and get us back under it.'

'Shall I cut it again, sir?'

As he asked, there was a sudden muffled

explosion from the direction of the *Tirpitz*.
Then another.

'Depth-charges!' exclaimed Stevens.

'They must have spotted the other X-craft!' I said with horror.

Chapter 13
Target!

The explosions continued behind us as the depth-charges dropped down around our sister X-craft.

'Quick, Watson,' I ordered, 'get out there. Don't waste time cutting anything, just pull up that net and let's get under it! We'll take a chance on the buoys moving. With a bit of luck the surface will be boiling so much from their depth charges that the Germans won't notice.'

While Stevens kept us on course and I kept watch through the periscope, Munro once more helped Watson into the W & D room. It was all done at speed, there was no time to be lost. The minutes to the explosion were still ticking away. Twenty-seven ... twenty-six ... twenty-five ...

From behind us the sound of depth-charges going off still reverberated through the water.

It seemed to take for ever, but at last the W & D room filled with water and the outer hatch opened. Watson swam out to the anti-torpedo net. He moved upwards, hauling the net with him. Although the water helped reduce the weight of the metal mesh, it was still very heavy.

'Take her to two knots,' I ordered. 'Keep her low.'

Stevens and Munro worked feverishly at their controls to keep X11 on a straight and level course, despite being rocked by after-shocks coming through the water. We moved under the net, our hull scraping on the bed of the fjord as before. Instinctively I checked my watch. Twenty minutes before the blast.

There was a terrible metalic crash from outside as the heavy net became too much for Watson and he dropped it on to the top of the sub. For a second I was worried that it would get tangled up in our propeller . . . but then we were clear.

'Right, get Watson back in double-quick!'
I snapped.

Munro was already at the door of the W
& D room, watching for Watson's raised
thumb to appear to let us know he was in
and the outer hatch was shut.

'He's in, skipper,' he reported.

'Good. Open number two vents and
Kingston, and get that door open.'

A few moments later Watson was back
inside, panting with exhaustion.

'Full speed ahead,' I ordered.

'Full speed ahead it is, skipper,' said
Stevens.

My watch now showed eleven minutes to
detonation. I wondered what had happened to the crew of the X-craft that had
been depth-charged. And what about the
third midget sub? Was that in the Kaafjord
with us?

Ten minutes to go.

The depth-charging had ceased. Did that
mean the Germans were now coming to
look for us?

'Maintain five knots.'

'Five knots it is, sir.'

Five minutes to go. Four. Three.

Through the cloudy water I could just make out the large mesh net of the boom that separated us from the waters of Altenfjord, and the Atlantic beyond. The boom was firmly down, trapping us inside Kaafjord. I guessed that even as we were trying to get away, German reinforcement boats were on their way to scour the fjord for other subs.

My watch showed one minute to go . . . then zero . . . and nothing happened. The charges had failed to detonate.

My three crewmen had been studying their watches as well and looks of despair crossed their faces. Especially Munro's, who'd come on this mission in memory of his brother, and now saw it turning into another disaster.

'What d'you reckon's gone wrong, skipper?' asked Stevens.

I sighed heavily. 'Perhaps –'

And then there was the sound of a terrific explosion way back behind us, followed by another, and then another. Our X-craft was hurled through the water.

We fought to right her again, desperate to keep her from going into the anti-submarine net beneath the boom.

As Munro, Stevens and Watson cheered and shook hands with each other, I said: 'Looks like we've done it. Now all we have to do is get away.'

Chapter 14

Short of Oxygen

With our mission accomplished, we now had to get out of the fjords and make our rendezvous with the *Saracen*. Once more Bill Watson went out and cut the bottom part of the boom net so that we were able to slip under it. It was a tight squeeze and only a midget submarine could have done it. I guessed most of the Germans' attention was on the *Tirpitz*. If we'd damaged her as badly as I hoped we had, then all available hands would be busy picking up survivors.

Watson rejoined us back out in Altenfjord.

'Right,' I ordered. 'Out to the open sea. Course five four three.'

'Course five four three it is, sir,' repeated Stevens.

By now the air in X11 was starting to get pretty thick. It had been many hours since we'd had a chance to surface and open the hatch to get some fresh air in. The build up of carbon dioxide would get to us soon, and there was a serious danger of us making mistakes. I was aware that all four of us were beginning to pant heavily – one of the first symptoms of oxygen starvation. We were breathing in mainly carbon dioxide. Unless we surfaced soon, the next stage would be dizziness, followed by drowsiness, and finally sleep – a sleep from which we wouldn't wake up.

Stevens was already showing the first signs of excessive carbon dioxide: his eyelids were drooping and his head kept jerking up as he fought to keep himself awake. For myself, I could feel a fog starting to cloud my brain and hamper decision-making. It was even becoming difficult to keep my eyes focused. Bill Watson was the least affected, mainly because he'd recently been taking in oxygen while swimming outside.

'Watson,' I said, 'how much oxygen is left in your tank?'

'About enough for one more dive, skipper.'

I weighed it up. If we shared the oxygen around now, it would all be gone and if we ran into any underwater obstacles, there'd be no way of getting past them because we'd have no diver.

On the other hand, we had the floating minefield in Altenfjord to get through. If we attempted to do it while we were in a confused state, there was every likelihood that we'd hit one of the mine's detonating spines and blow ourselves up.

Our third option was to surface now. But if we did that we'd be caught for sure. The fjords must be crawling with Germans on full alert.

I reached my decision. 'We're going to pass round Watson's oxygen. Don't breathe too deeply. Two shallow breaths each first. Then we'll pass it round again. Hopefully it will keep our heads clear until we're through the minefield. After that, we'll surface as soon as it's safe.'

I took in my two breaths slowly and carefully. The fuzziness in my head began to clear at once. The others also seemed to become that little bit more alert. The oxygen went round again. Watson took the last turn and then checked the amount of oxygen left.

'There's maybe enough for one person to have another shot,' he announced. 'But not enough for me to go out again.'

'OK, let's hope we don't have to stay under any longer than we need,' I said.

I had decided to set our return course through the minefield. It was dangerous, but it would give us cover. Anyway, we'd done it before and survived. I looked through the periscope and saw the forest of cables that anchored the floating mines, dead ahead of us.

'OK,' I said. 'Steady as we go.'

'Steady as we go, sir,' echoed Stevens.

Coming through the minefield had been difficult enough on our journey up through Altenfjord. Now, even after the shots of oxygen, we were still feeling light-headed. I had to concentrate hard as I gave instructions to Stevens.

'Ten degrees starboard.'

We changed our course just enough for us to slip in between two cables. We were in shallow water now and I could see through the viewing port the dangerous spines of the mines above us. They seemed even closer to us than on our inbound journey. If I hadn't been suffering from lack of oxygen I would have made the connection much sooner – of course, the tide! On this return journey the water level was lower than it had been on our way in.

'Depth?' I asked.

'Twenty feet, sir,' said Munro.

Twenty feet! We had come up on a shelf rising in the middle of the fjord. I could see the long spines of the mines barely inches above us. If we even just so much as scraped one, we'd be dead.

'Keep her steady,' I said. 'Five degrees to port.'

We scrambled along the sea-bed.

'Depth?' I asked.

'Nineteen feet, sir,' responded Munro.

We were rising, forced by the ebbing tide. Any second now we'd be right up among the mines. I wondered whether I should try and get us out of the minefield, but the forest of cables was all around us. It was one thing trying to snake through them; it would be quite another to attempt to turn through ninety degrees surrounded by cables. We'd be bound to snag on one and pull a mine down on to us.

It looked as if we were stuck, with no way forward and no way back.

Chapter 15

Going Down

'Keep her steady,' I murmured.

Inside X11 all was quiet bar the hum of the motor and our breathing as we moved slowly forward.

'Depth?'

'Still nineteen feet, sir,' replied Munro. 'No, twenty. Twenty-two. Twenty-four.' He looked up as his face broke into a grin of relief. 'We've passed the shelf, sir! It's getting deeper again.'

Once clear of the minefield I waited until we were far enough along Altenfjord for it to be safe to surface. I ordered us up to periscope depth and took a careful check around. This far from Kaafjord the area seemed to be clear. There were no vessels visible on the surface. I also couldn't see any enemy lookout posts on the fjord's sheer cliff sides.

'OK, blow tube,' I ordered.

'Tube blown, sir,' said Munro.

We rose to the surface.

'Careful as you open the hatch,' I warned.

We all knew of cases where the hatch had been opened too quickly and the carbon dioxide build-up had led to it exploding out, hurling the man who opened the hatch into the sea. Fortunately this didn't happen. The smell of fresh air was the sweetest smell we could have experienced.

'OK, ten minutes' break before we continue on our way,' I said, and we all took turns to breathe in the air.

We were running seriously behind schedule. As we approached the open North Atlantic it was almost 2000 hours, the time scheduled for our rendezvous. I calculated that we still had at least another three hours' journey time. Commander Perry had promised he would give us until 2200 hours, but then he would have to leave. At this rate we would arrive one hour late. However, we had no choice but to push on and hope that the fleet might give us a bit more leeway.

At 2215 hours we were still three miles short of the rendezvous position.

'We're going to miss them,' moaned Watson in desperation. 'All this way and we're going to miss them!'

'We're going to be stuck if we do,' said Munro. 'We can hardly sail this thing across the North Atlantic. We haven't got enough fuel to travel more than twenty miles past the pick-up point.'

'In which case we'll just have to sit and wait until the Germans arrive and pick us up,' I said.

'*If* they pick us up,' commented Stevens. 'After what we did to the *Tirpitz* they're more likely to bomb us than rescue us.'

'Let's take a chance and travel on the surface,' I snapped in exasperation. 'We'll be able to go faster and we might catch them.'

'Unless they've gone already,' pointed out Watson. 'They were only supposed to wait until 2000. We're two hours late already.'

'True,' I said 'But we've got nothing to lose. Take her up.'

Once on the surface I opened the hatch and scanned the sea ahead through my binoculars. Nothing. No sign of the S-subs. It was possible they were still there, but submerged. Without a radio, though, we couldn't reach them.

'Full speed ahead,' I ordered, 'and keep your fingers crossed.'

'Full speed ahead it is, skipper,' said Stevens.

And so we sailed across that vast open expanse, our tiny craft heading into the open North Atlantic. Through my binoculars I looked for any sign of the other subs. The moon was full and I could see for miles. Still nothing.

Suddenly I heard the drone of a plane's engine behind me. I turned and my heart sank. Coming towards us was a Dornier bomber, unmistakable in the moonlit sky.

I hastily dropped back down inside the midget sub and slammed the hatch shut.

'What is it, skipper?' asked Stevens.

'We've got company!' I shouted. 'A German bomber. *Dive!*'

Munro and Watson swung into action, opening the valves and filling our tanks with ballast while Stevens kept watch on the controls and I took my position at the periscope.

The first depth-charges exploded in the sea around us just as we were going down.

Unfortunately for us, the moon had provided the Dornier with a perfect sighting of us.

Our hull creaked and groaned, and then suddenly water began to pour in from above the periscope housing.

'Hull's been breached!' shouted Munro.

Water cascaded down on to the main control panel. Sparks flew and it caught alight. Smoke began to fill the inside of the sub. We were also nearly up to our knees in water and sinking fast.

We had only one choice – to abandon ship. And we had to do it quickly, before we went down with her.

'Take her up!' I ordered. Better to take our chances with the bomber than drown.

By the time we reached the surface the water was waist-deep and the smoke was choking and blinding us. Just as I was about to lose consciousness I managed to get the hatch open. I hauled myself out on to the tiny deck. Watson followed me, then Munro, then Stevens.

Squeezed for space, we clung to the hull and tried to get a foot-hold to stop ourselves from falling into the sea. With the heavy clothing we wore to protect us from the cold, we'd sink like stones if we fell in.

We heard the rattle of machine-gun fire and tensed, expecting the bullets to tear into us at any second. Instead there was a sudden dull *WHOOOMPF* from above. I looked up to see one of the Dornier's wings burst into flames. For a second it hung in the sky. Then it spiralled into the sea on our port side in a cloud of smoke and flames.

'There!' shouted Munro, pointing.

I turned and saw the shape of a submarine on the surface about half a mile away to starboard, the machine-gun on its deck still pointing upwards. As I watched another sub rose from beneath the sea, its conning tower breaking against the waves. The *Saracen*!

Beneath us X11 was sinking fast. The

sea was now up to our waists. Just before our tiny craft went down, the *Saracen* came alongside us and we scrambled on to it, doing our best to get a grip on the slippery hull. Eager hands grabbed us and hauled us aboard.

Once down below, Commander Perry shook each of us by the hand. 'Well done, all of you. According to our initial intelligence, the *Tirpitz* has had it.'

'Just now we thought we'd had it too, sir,' I said.

'To be honest, we'd just about given you up,' Perry said. 'Luckily we picked up the Dornier depth-charging something, and we knew it had to be you, so we came back.'

'What about the other X-crafts, sir?' I asked. 'Any news of them?'

Perry's face grew grave. 'Up to now, I'm afraid you're the only ones to make it back. If they were lucky, the Germans will have taken them prisoner. If not . . .'

He left the sentence unfinished. We all understood. That was war.

'Now,' said Perry, 'get yourselves a hot drink, something to eat and some kip. It's a long way home.'

Author's Note

Although this is a fictional story, it is based on real events, but the names have been changed.

In the actual attack on the *Tirpitz*, six X-craft – X5, X6, X7, X8, X9 and X10 – set out from Scotland for Norway, each towed by a large parent-submarine.

X8 and X9 were lost at sea on the outward journey. The other four reached Norway. They were commanded by Lt. Henty-Creer (X5), Lt. D. Cameron (X6), Lt. B. C. G. Place (X7) and Lt. K. R. Hudspeth (X10), an Australian Reserve officer.

X10 suffered major electrical failures as well as serious leaks and had to abandon her attack. She was able to make the rendezvous with one of the parent-submarines and began her journey back to Scotland. However, because of gales, X10 was scuttled before she reached base.

X6 penetrated the net around the German battleship but was spotted. However, the crew managed to release the charges before scuttling the X-craft. Lt. Cameron and his men were taken on board the *Tirpitz* as prisoners.

X7 became entangled in the net protecting the *Tirpitz*, came under fire and sank. Only Lt. Place and the diver survived, and they were also taken prisoner.

X5 was subjected to a barrage from German armaments and disappeared. No trace of her or her four-man crew was ever found.

What Happened Next?

The *Tirpitz* was not sunk by the explosive charges laid beneath it by the X-craft, but she was very badly damaged. All of her three main turbines were disabled, as were her generators, electrical equipment, port rudder and range-finders. The huge crippled ship lay out of action in the Norwegian fjord for six months while engineers worked to repair her.

This gave the RAF time to plan a final assault on the ship. On 3 April 1944 a force of carrier-based aircraft bombed the *Tirpitz*. This caused such serious damage that she was unable to be repaired except in a fully equipped shipyard. So the *Tirpitz* was moved south to Tromso to be used as a floating coastal battery. Here she was finally sunk on 12 November 1944 by a force of Lancaster bombers using 12,000 lb Tallboy bombs.

Was it worth it?

The *Tirpitz* being put out of action by the X-craft had a threefold effect:

• The vital supply convoys from Britain to Russia could continue in greater safety.

• The sinking of the *Tirpitz* put an end to the belief that the German Navy was invincible and in control of the North Atlantic.

• A significant number of ships in the British Navy were released to engage the enemy in other theatres of war, instead of being restricted to the North Atlantic.

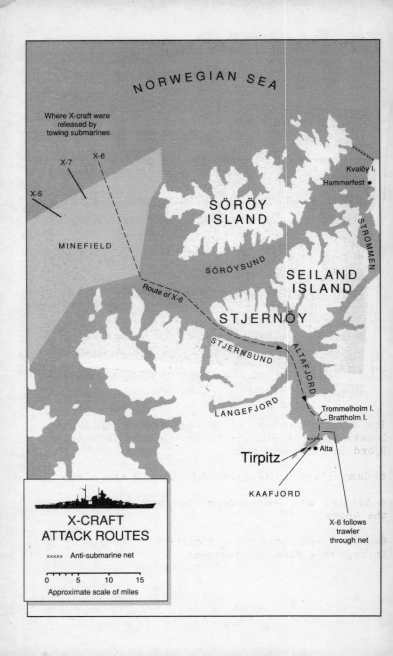

Tirpitz in Norway

The *Tirpitz* was moored in various Norwegian locations. This picture shows the ship in the Ass Fjord in February 1942.

● Camouflage units surround the bow and stern.

● Netting was draped from the vessel's portside to the shore.

● Additional mines made *Tirpitz* a virtually impregnable floating fortress.

Inside the X-craft

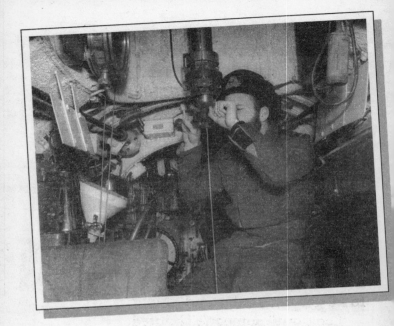

This photograph was classified until its release in 1945.

● Space was extremely limited.

● The periscope provided the only link with the outside world.

● The 'steering' wheel can be seen in the left-hand corner.

● Comforts were few and far between, but note the hot-water urn behind the chair on the left-hand side.

What was it like to be a naval gunner in the Second World War? Find out for yourself in the next *Warpath* adventure, *Last Convoy*

Suddenly, there was an explosion towards the foredeck. The ship shuddered and I saw a mass of water cascading down on to the deck. Above the noise I could hear the howl of a dive-bomber's engine. It seemed to be getting louder and louder.

'Look out!' someone shouted.

I spun round and saw the Stuka bearing down on us. The starboard Oerlikons, Brownings and Bofors had engaged the plane but it continued towards us, regardless of the fire coming at it. It was a battle of wills – he wasn't giving up and neither were we. The aircraft was now dangerously close but still it came down without a hint that it would pull up from its dive.

'Get down!' shouted Bill. 'He's going to crash aboard!'

We flung ourselves to the deck. It shook violently as the Stuka smashed into our foredeck. As the smoke cleared I could see a wing resting against the bridge, like a dead bird. Inside the shattered canopy were the goggled figures of the pilot and his rear gunner – both of them were obviously dead. Petrol gushed over the deck from the plane's ruptured tanks. The firefighters sprang into action at once, using the deck water lines to swill it over the side.

'That was a lucky escape!' exclaimed Bill.

We approached the wreckage cautiously.

'Watch out!' shouted a voice. 'It's still got a bomb attached!'

Everyone stopped dead in their tracks. Maybe we hadn't been so lucky. Jack Holder appeared with his armourer's kit. He was probably the only man aboard who could handle the situation.

'Right,' he said. 'I need two volunteers. Now!'

Everyone looked round, shuffling their feet nervously.

'I'll have a go,' said Bill, as he moved forward.

Jack shook his head. 'Not you, chum. You're the only other armourer aboard and there's no way we can both take the risk. Come on, someone else.'

'Count me in.' I heard myself speak before I realized what I was doing.

WARPATH

Following in the footsteps of fighting heroes

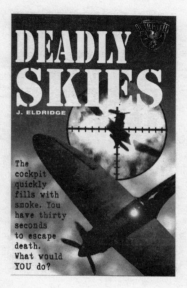

August 1940 — Britain stands alone against the might of the Nazi blitzkrieg. Across the English Channel, just twenty miles away, enemy forces prepare to invade. For one young pilot the Battle of Britain is about to begin.

Part war story, part fact book, *Deadly Skies* reveals what it was really like to fly a plane and fight in the Battle of Britain.

Collect the set

Following in the footsteps of fighting heroes

January 1943 — The Japanese seem invincible in the jungles of South-East Asia. But one man believes otherwise, and he sends 3000 Chindit soldiers on a mission behind enemy lines. The catch is, as one young officer discovers, there is no planned escape route.

Part war story, part fact book, *Behind Enemy Lines* reveals what it was really like to take part in a commando mission during the Second World War.

Collect the set

Following in the footsteps of fighting heroes

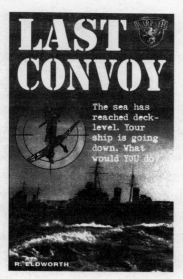

August 1942 — Malta lies under siege.
Its capture would wreck the Allied North
African campaign. In a final bid to save
the island, a last convoy is despatched
with vital supplies.

Part war story, part fact book, *Last
Convoy* reveals what it was like to be
a gunner on board the fortified
merchant ship *Ohio*.

Available from January 2000

Following in the
footsteps of
fighting heroes

If you have enjoyed reading this
Warpath book we would like to
hear from you. Let us know what
you enjoyed most about the story.
Give us your suggestions for other
titles. Make comments as to how
we can make the series better.

Send your letters to:

Dept NH
Puffin Books
27 Wrights Lane
London
W8 5TZ